FRIENDSHIPS
AND
BULLYING

HONOR HEAD

W
FRANKLIN WATTS
LONDON • SYDNEY

Franklin Watts
First published in Great Britain in 2020
by The Watts Publishing Group
Copyright © The Watts Publishing Group, 2020

Editor: Amy Pimperton
Designers: Peter Scoulding and Cathryn Gilbert
Cover design: Peter Scoulding
Consultant: Clare Arnold, psychotherapist with 25 years'
experience working with CAMHS, the NHS's Child and
Adolescent Mental Health Services

HB ISBN: 978 1 4451 7113 5
PB ISBN: 978 1 4451 7114 2

FSC
www.fsc.org
MIX
Paper from
responsible sources
FSC® C104740

Printed and bound in Dubai

Picture credits:
Shutterstock: Kurit Afshen 27t, 28l; andamanec 22b;
AndreAnita 15t; ArCalu 23r; Agnieszka Bacal 17c; Natalia
Bachkova 2, 14, 30c; Masha Basova 27b; Henk Bentlage
4; Uwe Bergwitz 6; un.bolovan 21b; Ryan M Bolton 25cl;
borgil 29t; Ekaterina Brusnika 11b; Ken Calderhead 19b;
Abhay Chaware 19t; Phuwadon Chulasukhont 29cr;
Belle Ciezak 23l, 32; Danita Delmont 26; dezy 7cl, 15bl,
30t; Celso Diniz 7tr; Alexander Ermolaev front cover;
fontoknak 15cr; gadag 5cl, 30b; Giedrius 11c; Joe Gough
9bc; Pascale Gueret 7br; Miroslav Halama 20; hiopex 13b;
Eric isselee 13t; Ammit Jack 5tr; Kletr 18; knelson 19c;
Grigorita Ko 8c; Panagiotis Komninelis 25r; Steve Lagreca
12; Rich Lindie 24b; Lubava 17t; Natalia Lukiyanova
11t; marima 9tr; Katho Menden 16; MizKitty 21c; Nagel
Photography 9l; Kelly Nelson 28-29b; Noheapphotos 27c;
panda3800 22t; PIPPO-CHI 17b; Ondrej Prosicky 5br, 21t;
Villiers Steyn 24t; Tap10 13c; Dwi Yulianto 10.

Franklin Watts, an imprint of
Hachette Children's Group
Carmelite House
50 Victoria Embankment
London EC4Y 0DZ

An Hachette UK Company
www.hachette.co.uk
www.franklinwatts.co.uk

Contents

What is friendship? 4

Everyone needs friends 6

Making new friends 8

Being unfriendly 10

What kind of friend are you? 12

Friendships take work 14

Enjoy sharing 16

Be kind 18

Stand up for yourself 20

Friendships change 22

Bullying 24

Making friends online 26

Online bullying 28

Be resilient! 30

Notes for parents, carers and teachers 31

Glossary, websites and index 32

Everyone faces challenging times in their life. This book will help you to develop the resilience skills you need to cope with difficult situations in all areas of life.

What does it mean to build resilience?

When we build resilience we can better cope with things, such as being bullied or losing a friend. Building resilience means we accept that times are difficult now, but that we can and will get back to enjoying life. Learning how to build resilience is a valuable life skill.

What is a trusted adult?

A trusted adult is anyone that you trust and who makes you feel safe. It can be a parent or carer, a relative or a teacher. If you have no one you want to talk to, phone a helpline (see page 32).

What is friendship?

Friendship is about sharing. Not just sharing things, but sharing your time and your feelings. When you share, you make people feel special and cared for. Sharing also makes you feel good about yourself.

Sharing is fun and makes everyone feel happy.

When you have resilience you can bounce back from bad things. When you feel good about yourself and have friends that care about you, this helps you to be resilient when you feel sad or afraid.

A special friend is someone that you can turn to. A friend who trusts you helps your self-esteem and confidence. Friends can help you to build up your resilience, or inner strength, to help you cope at difficult times.

If someone bullies you, shouts at you, is rude or nasty and does not care how they make you feel, that is not a true friend. Good friends look after each other.

Everyone needs friends

Finding a good friend is very special. Friends are people you enjoy being with. They make you feel happy. Friends help you through the bad times and are with you to enjoy the good times.

Friends can be like you or completely different.

Friends cheer you up when you feel sad. They are there to give you a hug, hold your hand or just listen. A real friend is someone who tries to understand how you feel.

Being with friends can be exciting and fun. Just spending quiet time together can feel special, too. Friends help to make happy memories you will have forever. Happy memories help you to bounce back when you are going through difficult times.

A true friend never laughs at you or makes you feel silly. Good friends always say sorry if they upset you.

Making new friends

Take a deep breath and look forward to meeting new people.

You will meet new people and make new friends all your life. Making friends can be a bit scary, but remember everyone feels a bit nervous meeting new people. Smile and be polite and friendly and most people will behave the same way to you.

Talk to a trusted adult if you feel anxious about meeting new people. We are all different in many ways, but inside nearly everyone wants to be liked and loved.

Lots of us feel shy about meeting others. Look for someone who is standing alone or being quiet. Smile and say 'hello'. They probably feel shy, too. Feeling shy is okay.

Asking questions shows that you want to be friends. Make sure you listen to the answer without interrupting.

Being unfriendly

Not everyone will want to be friendly and there is nothing you can do about this. If some people don't want to be friends, stay positive and try again with other people.

Remember that if someone does not want to be your friend it is not because of you.

You do not have to change who you are to make friends. Be proud of who you are and be yourself. Accept others for the way they are, too.

If others ignore you, whisper behind your back or leave you out of things, this is a form of bullying. Tell a trusted adult if you are being bullied. Try not to let what other people say upset you and look for other friends.

Some people like to have lots of friends, some like to have one or two best friends. How many friends you have is not important. What is important is to have friends you can trust and who make you feel safe and loved.

11

What kind of friend are you?

Are you loyal and helpful or bossy and mean? Do you listen or only think about what you want to say? Are you happy when your friends have good luck or do something well or do you feel a bit jealous?

There are lots of ways to make sure you are a good friend.

Think of ways to help and support your friends. Let your friends know you are there to listen to them. Tell them you will help them work out any problems.

Be happy for your friends when something good happens to them. There is no reason to feel jealous. When your turn comes it will be great to have friends who feel happy for you.

Take a deep breath before you say something that might upset someone. Think about how you would feel if someone said the same thing to you.

If you feel angry or jealous, talk to a trusted adult about it. Don't let these feelings grow and get worse. They might make you say or do nasty or mean things.

Friendships take work

To make a friendship work we need trust, loyalty, respect and forgiveness. We need to try to understand how other people feel. This is called empathy.

We trust friends and feel safe with them.

Friends don't have to agree about everything. Even close friends can have disagreements. Respect what other people think and say as long as it is not hurting anyone.

If you have an argument with a friend and it is your fault, say sorry.

If your friend has upset you, try not to shout or get angry. Maybe there is a good reason for what happened. Talk about it to understand the problem and be friends again.

Enjoy sharing

Sharing with other people makes you feel good about yourself. Learning how to share and take turns can be difficult. It can be hard to give something to someone else when you want to keep it.

Sharing helps us to play and work together as a team.

If your friend wants to share something, such as a toy, talk about a fair way to share it. You could agree to take it in turns to have the toy for 10 minutes each.

While you are waiting for your turn, think about other things you can do. You might find something more interesting to do. Sometimes we only want something because someone else has it, not because we really want it.

If your best friend spends time with another person it can make you feel jealous, hurt and angry. But think, if your friend likes someone else, you might like them, too. Join in and see if you can all be friends.

Be kind

Being kind is when you do or say things to help others. Doing something kind makes people feel good. It makes people smile. You should be kind to everyone, not just your friends.

Being kind to others helps you to feel good about yourself.

When we feel angry or that something is unfair, we might say something nasty rather than explain what we feel. If this happens, talk to your friend about why you feel bad.

If you do get angry or upset, think of something else. Bounce back by singing your favourite song. You could walk away or have a drink of water until the feeling passes.

If someone is unkind to you, it is okay to feel angry or sad, but do not be unkind back. Crying is a natural way to let out your feelings. You are not being silly or a baby.

Stand up for yourself

If you have a friend who is very bossy or doesn't know how to share, don't get angry or sulky. Talk to your friend and say that you are not happy with what is going on.

Sometimes, bossy people won't want to listen to others.

Talk to a trusted adult about what to say to your friend. Perhaps role play the scene — the adult can pretend to be your friend.

Take a deep breath and tell your friend how you feel. Don't shout or be rude. If your friend will not listen, walk away and try again another time.

If your friends say you are bossy, don't get angry or say you are not. Think about your behaviour. Talk to a grown-up you trust about it. Maybe you are bossy and you don't realise it.

Friendships change

Sometimes a good friend may not want to be best friends any more. Or you may meet another person you want to be friends with. This is okay. Some friendships will last for a very long time, others will not.

When a friendship ends you may think that you did something wrong. Unless your friend has said you did something to upset them, do not blame yourself for what has happened.

Accepting that friendships end can help you bounce back when they do.

If you lose a friend you may feel lonely and angry. It is okay to feel sad and cry. Talk about how you feel or write down your feelings. The bad feeling will pass.

As you grow up, sometimes friends grow apart and want to do different things. Losing a friend happens to everyone. Talk to your family about it, have a hug and look for new friends.

Bullying

Some people are bullies. They don't like to share, are rude and say nasty things. Some bullies hurt people by hitting, scratching, pulling hair, pushing or doing other mean things.

Stay away from people that bully you or upset you.

If you are being bullied, it is not your fault. No one deserves to be bullied. Keep away from the bully if you can. Do not be mean or rude back.

Talk to an adult you trust straight away about anyone who is bullying you. You do not have to put up with being bullied.

Are you a bully? Think about why you bully others. Build resilience by talking to someone about your behaviour and how you can change it. People are there to support you and help you to understand why you bully others.

Making friends online

Soon you may start to make friends online. Making digital friends is different from real-life friends as you cannot see the people you are talking to.

Being online is fun and exciting, but you have to be careful.

Online it is easy for people to pretend to be kind and friendly, even if they are not like that at all. Do not give your full name, address, age, your school, name or address or any details about friends or family to anyone online.

Some people may lie about who they are or ask you to keep secrets. They might say things that upset and frighten you. If this happens, turn off the device and tell a trusted adult straight away.

Don't forget your real-life friends. Digital friends cannot give you a hug or a real smile.

Online bullying

Online bullying is called cyberbullying. In the future you will meet lots of new people online, but not all of them will be nice. Some people will be rude and nasty. Ignore these people.

Find sites online that make you feel happy.

People online often say mean things because they do not have to face the person they are bullying. Bounce back by remembering that you have real friends and family who care about you.

On some sites you may post pictures that others have to 'like'. Remember you don't need online likes to feel good about yourself. If you like the picture you posted, that is all that matters.

If people say nasty things about anything you post online, just switch off. Read a book, listen to music or plan to meet real-life friends.

Be resilient!

Being resilient means being able to cope with times when you feel sad or are going through a situation that makes you feel afraid or anxious. Here is a reminder of how friendships are a great way to help you become resilient.

- Friends can make you feel cared for and supported. They can help build your confidence and self-esteem.

- Having the support of friends gives you the confidence to try new things, explore and be adventurous.

- Having friends that come to you for support when they feel sad or upset makes you feel worthwhile. Hugging a sad friend makes you feel good and helps your friend.

- We have to learn to accept it when friends don't want to be friendly any more. We learn that this is not our fault and find new friends. This will help you to bounce back from feeling sad.

- It is important to learn the difference between good and bad friends. Bad friends are bullies and make us feel small and unhappy. We should still be kind to mean people, but not allow them to hurt us.

Notes for parents, carers and teachers

There are many ways parents, carers and teachers can help children develop resilience skills through friendships.

Encourage children to be adventurous, to experiment and try new things. Reinforce that failure is not a bad thing, but can be very positive. Having fun and having a go is more important than doing it right.

By trying new things, children are more likely to meet a wide range of people, which will increase their social skills and build a network of friends.

Talk to children about friendships and what friends mean to them. Discuss how they treat friends and how they expect friends to treat them.

Talk about the differences between good and bad friendships. Discuss how their behaviour affects others and vice versa.

Role play different friendship scenarios: having a row, being mean, refusing to share, losing a friend. How does it make them feel? Discuss ways to cope with negative feelings.

Discuss with children the ways that they can control a friendship: by being kind, thoughtful and helpful, and not allowing others to bully them. Discuss the ways that they cannot control a friendship, for example, a friend going off with someone else or not sharing. Having control builds confidence. Learning and accepting that we cannot control other people builds resilience.

Read through this book. Talk about the topics on each page. Role play a situation relating to the topic.

Finally, not all children will have or want lots of friends, some may just have one or two special friends. Some children prefer to spend time by themselves. All children are different, so don't force friendships on a child. However, if you feel your child is being anti-social or seems to be isolated from others, talk to the child and see if there is an underlying reason, such as bullying or excessive anxiety. Don't feel ashamed or silly about talking to a doctor or teacher about the situation if you think this will help.

Glossary

anxious feeling worried or nervous about how something is going to turn out

bossy someone who likes to tell others what to do

confidence believing you are good at doing things

forgiveness to stop being angry with someone for something that they did

jealous being angry or upset if someone has something you want

loyalty helping and supporting someone

nervous feeling scared or worried about something

respect to be kind and understanding about how another person thinks or feels

role play to act out a situation by pretending to be the people involved

self-esteem believing you are good enough to do things well

trust to believe that someone is reliable and truthful

Websites

These sites have information on friendship and bullying issues.

www.childline.org.uk/info-advice/bullying-abuse-safety/types-bullying
Children's helpline: 0800 1111
www.cyh.com/HealthTopics/HealthTopicDetailsKids.aspx?p=335&np=286&id=1636
www.kidshealth.org/en/kids/talkingabout-friends.html
www.youngminds.org.uk
Parents' helpline: 0808 802 5544

Index

anxiety 8, 30

confidence 5, 30
crying 19, 23

disagreements 15

empathy 14

hugs 7, 23, 27, 30

jealousy 12, 13, 17

laughing 7
listening 7, 9, 12, 20, 21, 29

saying sorry 7, 15
self-esteem 5, 30
shyness 9